The Bowery Butcher

By

Daryl Parker

BALCONY BOOKS

This story is a work of fiction. References to real people, events, establishments, organizations or locales are intended only to provide a sense of authenticity, and are used fictitiously. All other characters and all incidents and dialogue are drawn from the author's imagination and are not to be construed as real.

THE BOWERY BUTCHER. Copyright © 2015 by Daryl Parker, all rights reserved. Published and printed in the United States of America. No part of this book may be used or reproduced in any manner whatsoever without written permission except in the case of brief quotations embodied in critical articles and reviews.

Balcony Books may be purchased for educational, business, or sales promotional use.

FIRST BALCONY BOOKS EDITION, PUBLISHED 2015.

Copyright © 2015 Daryl Parker
All rights reserved.
ISBN-10: 1522975225
ISBN-13: 978-1522975229

DEDICATION

To my wife Jennifer, who continues to inspire and motivate me every day.

New York City, circa 1859

The girl blinked, which surprised him because he had thought she was already dead. It was hard to tell in the musty dankness of the cellar. She lay on the floor, her mouth working like a fish in the bottom of a boat. Too late to throw her back though, she was beyond help, and Nicholas knew it. He crawled closer. Her eyes were still alive, but there was no awareness beyond an ebbing fixation on some hidden vision. He reached for her pale hand, but a black ooze chased him back. The viscous liquid only looked black in the dark. It was actually a sticky, warm, copper and iron red, and it wouldn't do to get any of it on him. A hoarse cough drifted down from upstairs, and he scuttled back to his corner.

"Hey there, Detective, are you alright?" Sergeant Shay placed a hand on his shoulder to steady him.

"What? Yes, I'm fine." Nicholas shook off the memories.

"Well, what's this now, three?"

"Four." *That we know of anyway*, he thought. The woman's naked body was tied to a chair, bound at the wrists and ankles. A rope ran underneath her breasts and secured her in an upright position. Like the other victims, her genitalia was a mess of flesh cut to ribbons.

Thickening blood puddled on the floor beneath her and her chin rested on her chest, long hair obscuring the face. Nicholas used his cane for support as he knelt to look at the ruin. Thin trails of dried blood ran from raw, empty eye sockets, and her lips were bubbled and puckered by heavy stitches that pulled them tightly together.

"Can you light that other lamp there as well? I need more light." Sergeant Shay did as he was bid and held the oil lamp for Nicholas. The landlady had already been through the apartment before they arrived and doubtlessly removed any valuables. Judging from the smears of blood on the floor, several other gawkers had probably traipsed through the crime scene as well.

"What a mess. This is a nasty bastard, that's for sure." The sergeant shook his head.

"Yes. Sergeant please jot a few notes for me." Shay put the lamp down and fished out a small notepad and stubby pencil. "Blood pooling in lower extremities indicate victim was already bound in the chair at the time of death; however, the minimal bleeding from eyes, mouth and genitals suggests mutilation occurred post-mortem." The sergeant's eyebrows raised and he continued, "The pooling of blood underneath the chair is drainage from her trunk, expressed through her wounds."

He took several minutes to look over the rest of her

body, but no other serious wounds were visible. "Blood loss didn't kill her, so the cause of death is here." Gently lifting sodden hair away from her temple revealed a flap of swollen skin covering a hole as big around as his thumb. He pulled a kerchief out of his pocket and wiped the blood off his fingers. Exactly like the others.

She had been killed by a sharp blow, probably a hammer. The abrupt trauma caused her hands to curl into tight claws. The coroner had termed this a "cadaveric spasm," a condition Nicholas knew well.

Her fingers reluctantly gave way to his prying. Small bits of blood lay under her fingernails. She had fought her assailant and scored him, but there was something else here. Held tightly in the grip of her right hand were a few strands of short hair, black and coarse with signs of graying at the ends. Most likely they were snatched from the killer's beard, giving Nicholas another clue to his identity. He pulled a small waxed envelope from his coat pocket and dropped the hairs inside.

"Alright Sergeant, I'm finished here." He looked at his pocket-watch; 11:30 pm. "Let them have her." Sergeant Shay waved the morgue-men in. The acme of efficiency, they simply threw a sheet over the woman before picking her up, chair and all, and carrying their charge out to a waiting wagon.

* * * * *

Detective Nicholas Cullen stumped down the sideboards of the Lower East Side. His mangled right foot made him useless in a foot-chase, but the residents here knew better than to count it against him. More than one thug had thought him an easy mark, only to receive cracked ribs and broken fingers from his brass-headed cane. As a member of the New York Municipal Police Department, he also carried a Colt revolver.

Back in his rooms above Lowry's hardware store, Nicholas stared at the clutter of papers scattered across his writing table. His bad foot was propped on a stool, and he picked absentmindedly at the bits of dried wax that peppered the tabletop. Wax was everywhere, on the floor, the bureau, even the walls. It was part of his study on the behavior of spilt blood, and while hogs-blood or ink would have upset his landlady, wax was an acceptable substitute. Nicholas spent many evenings slinging hot wax around his apartment and taking careful notes. His observations had contributed to his interpretation of this evening's crime scene. The human nether regions are full of major blood vessels, yet the pattern of the blood pooled beneath the victim was obviously not under the pressure of a beating heart.

The glass of scotch shook in his other hand, and he took a gulp before setting it on the table, pushing it away.

The bondage, the mutilation, the killing blow to the temple... *It is not possible. He is rotting on Blackwell's Island.*

That night Nicholas dreamed of the fish-girl again, but there were others as well. The dark-haired woman in the night robe made an appearance, as did the plump one who begged him to let her go.

He had tried. He did all she asked of him, tried to slip the chains around her ankles, but he could not free her before he heard the heavy thump of boots descending the stairs. It was too late to retreat, so he cowered, hiding his eyes from the worst of it. Each fresh shriek made him flinch, but eventually she fell silent. The man violated her carnally, his hoarse grunting a prelude to the quieter squishing sounds of flesh falling away from his carving knife. When it was over, Nicholas was punished for speaking to the girl. The ball-peen hammer smashed down on the top of his foot, crushing bones like twigs.

The nightmare startled Nicholas awake in a lightening dawn. Sweat had drenched his night clothes and slicked the hair to his forehead. His hands trembled, but a shot of scotch burned down his throat, righting him as he performed his morning toilet.

* * * * *

Nicholas waited in the darkness, fingering the revolver in his pocket. Six days had passed since the last murder and the tension was palpable. *He's hunting*, Nicholas thought. *I can feel him.*

His fellow detectives, Adams and McCarty, had nicknamed this killer the "Bowery Butcher" for his habit of mutilating his victims, who were all women in their twenties, living on the Lower East Side, but otherwise had nothing in common. Two were prostitutes, one a seamstress, and the last a housecleaner. Not until he marked the murder sites on a map did a pattern finally emerge.

"Dora Copeland, Hawthorne Street. Mary Crouch, 3rd Street." Nicholas placed pennies at the locations on the map. "Julia McConnell, Jacob Street, and Catherine Bosch, Henley Avenue."

"I'll be damned," whistled Adams, "I see it." The murders lined up over the Lower East Side like the four points of the compass and went in opposing order, North, South, East West. "What is the purpose of the order?"

"That's the question, isn't it?" said Nicholas. "I think he's trying to be clever, challenging us to keep up with him."

McCarty rubbed his chin. "So where is he headed next?"

Nicholas frowned. "If he continues this order, he'll most likely strike the Northeast section, but that's only a guess. We'll have to cover all four areas."

For the next five nights, the detectives rotated through each of the areas, hoping to prevent another killing.

This was the sixth night of their surveillance, and Nicholas was standing in an alleyway, eyeing passersby. It was after midnight, and he hoped that another night had been safely passed, but then, a loud bump, followed by a woman's raised voice. Nicholas drew his revolver and poked his head out of the alley. A crash of furniture and a muffled shriek came from the squalid tenement across the street. Rushing over to the ground level entrance that opened into a long unlit hallway lined with doors, he made his way quietly, listening for more sounds. With a lack of drainage, the daily filth of some four-hundred residents had soaked into the earth, rotting the building from the ground up. The stench in the lower levels was a hellish miasma that threatened to choke him, while the floorboards under his feet were spongey with rot.

Nicholas paused and strained his ears; nothing but the occasional murmur of conversation, or a chair scraping across a floor. The illumination from the street was dimmed when the silhouette of a burly man, wearing a cap and beard, appeared in the doorway. The big man walked towards him slowly, ponderously. *He's drunk,* Nicholas realized.

The odor of beer blew over him like a gale. "Eh, Vas? Wie bitte..." The German was counting doors, and Nicholas was apparently standing in front of his apartment.

"Sorry," he said, slipping the revolver back into his pocket and moving further down the hallway. Ten minutes passed with no further sounds. The disturbance was probably just a common marital argument, over as soon as it had begun. Nicholas returned to his patrol of the streets.

* * * * *

Detective McCarty nodded, "Alright then, can you tell me what he looked like?" The big German blew his nose into a kerchief.

"No, I cannot. It was very dark in here, as you can imagine." Voices floated out of the next apartment where Nicholas was examining the fifth victim.

The cupboard was overturned and a sugar dish had smashed on the floor.

Elizabeth Hamm was another prostitute, and she had been treated as roughly as the others, tied spread-eagle on her bed. The sheets were heavy with blood that pooled around the body and soaked through the thin straw mattress. The stench of voided bowels and death was only slightly more offensive than the noxious tenement smell.

Dammit! I was right outside this door! Nicholas gritted his teeth as McCarty walked in the room.

"The neighbor ran into him last night in the hall, but couldn't make him out."

"The big German?" McCarty nodded. "Nevermind that, it was me he ran into. I heard the struggle, but I couldn't pinpoint it."

"Hardly your fault Nick, just bad luck. We'll get him. Did you notice anyone enter the hall before the noises?"

"No, no one."

"Arrogant bastard, took his time didn't he? Stopped to eat." McCarty motioned to the remains of a meal on the spindly table.

Nicholas narrowed his eyes; the lone chair was turned around, the back butted up against the table.

* * * * *

"Lead on." The brute with the meaty hands lifted a brow, but turned and stalked down the hallway. A too-small bowler sat atop his rough, chopped haircut flanked by the cauliflower ears of a pugilist. The hulk led him through a rabbit's warren of turns to a heavy timbered door, which he tugged open with a large iron ring. Nicholas wanted to barge into the room and snatch Adain Bourke up by his collar, but he needed cooperation here.

"Mr. Bourke?" his guide inquired respectfully. "Cullen's here." Permission was granted and the thug pulled the door open.

The Mick, as he was known, sat behind a large desk chewing a mouthful of cheap beef. Gristle crunched and grease coated his shiny red lips. A mess of unruly red hair was haphazardly brushed to one side.

"Ah, Detective Cullen!" Bourke stood and whisked the checkered napkin from his collar to wipe his hands. His suit was snug, threatening to burst the buttons off his coat, as he stuck out a rough hand. Bourke was a powerfully built man, with a grip that was too hard to be polite, but Nicholas accepted it without response until Bourke released him.

"Hello Bourke."

"I was a bit surprised when I heard you wanted to speak to me. You've never been friendly before, you know. Have you come on hard times then? What can old Bourke do for you?"

"Nothing, I don't need anything. I'm here to help you."

"Help me? Now there's a change coming from a copper! You're all either trying to arrest me, or asking for money. What's your game?"

"No game, Bourke. Elizabeth Hamm was killed last night."

Bourke shrugged, "Don't know her, couldn't tell you anything about it."

"No doubt, but she was one of your girls, lived in the tenement on Park Drive."

"Park Drive..." Bourke's brow furrowed, "Oh, Liza! Yes, I know her. Well, knew her. Last night you say? What happened?"

He knew damn well what had happened. Bourke probably knew about the murder before the police did. "Someone's been killing your girls. I don't mean to tell you your business man, but she's the third prostitute killed in the past six weeks. Doesn't look good, if you know what I mean." Bourke looked him over shrewdly, smiling.

"Yes, Cullen, I take your meaning. Have you ever known me to neglect my affairs?"

"No. No, I haven't."

"Then as you said, why are you telling me my business?"

"Because in this case, your business is my business."

* * * * *

The backward chair kept coming to mind. His father use to sit in a backward chair, straddling the seat and folding his arms over the backrest, ready to spring to his feet.

The coach rattled over the cobblestone streets heading for the wharf. The roiling in his stomach irritated him, a sign of his nervousness. He hadn't seen his father in twenty-six years.

"Hello? Anyone down there?" A voice called down the stairs, but Nicholas didn't answer. No one ever came here unless they were brought here. He withdrew into the darkness under the stairs, hardly daring to breathe. Booted feet clumped down the steps, accompanied by the bright yellow light of a lantern. He didn't recognize the mustachioed man who came into view at the bottom of the stairs, but a silver star was pinned to his vest. He

held the lantern up, squinting around the room. "Oh my God."

Nicholas was a scrawny seven-year old when they found him tethered to the cellar wall. It was another two days before a doctor could remove the manacle around his ankle. The iron had rubbed his skin raw so many times that thick scar tissue had almost grown over it, like tree bark over a nail. There was nothing the doctor could do about the crushed bones in his foot except put it in a cast and hope for the best.

The shocking story of the boy chained in the cellar made all the papers, but Nicholas was just the sideshow, a tragic footnote to the story of his murderous father,

Josiah Cullen. The fish-girl had been the daughter of a wealthy family, who paid a hefty bounty to have her found. Nicholas was gently questioned, but he was unable to answer. The beatings, the starvation, the horrific sights and sounds; his father's cruelty had stolen his voice. Several months later his father was sentenced to life in prison, but Nicholas wanted to scream at them, *No! Kill him, kill him!*

The sensation passed and everyone went about their business. Perhaps some people wondered what happened to the little boy. His mother was only a faint memory, and with no other known relatives, he was sent to an orphanage.

The driver pulled the coach to a halt, the jangling traces mixing with waterfront sounds. "Your stop, Mister." Nicholas got out and wound his way through the waterfront bustle. A fat, battered prison tug bobbed at anchor, and he hailed the crew.

* * * * *

The stone apron of the prison on Blackwell's Island was covered in gull droppings and straw remnants of nests stuck out of every corner of the facade. The gate warden swung open the gate, and Nicholas stepped inside the thick stone walls.

The gate warden passed him off to a guard and they marched down long narrow hallways. He followed the guard into an inner court with two tiers of barred cells. Nicholas had been to several prisons, but today his palms were sweaty and his mouth was dry. *Steady, Nick!*

The guard came to the end of the row, and motioned to the last cell. "There he is. Do y'want the door open?"

"No." His breathing was quick as he stepped up to the bars. An indeterminate mound was lying on the narrow bed covered with a blanket. He cleared his throat,

"Josiah Cullen." He cursed the hitch in his voice as the figure sat up groggily.

"Whazzat?" A wrinkled, scrawny man pushed the blanket away and swung his feet to the floor. His wild hair was uncombed, and a large, bushy beard covered his face. Nicholas stood transfixed.

"Are you Josiah Cullen?"

"Who's asking?" No, no, the voice was wrong. It had been twenty-six years, but he knew the voice was different.

"Stand up!" Nicholas barked. The figure shrugged and stood, then began to laugh.

"Hee-hee-hee! He said you'd come for him! Damned if he wasn't right! Told me to look for a cripple." The man cackled again, a sparsely-toothed grin splitting his face.

"Open this door!" Nicholas ordered, and the guard quickly worked the lock and swung the door open. Nicholas rushed in and grabbed the man by his shirt.

"Where is Josiah Cullen?!"

The man cackled even louder, "Looking for your daddy, boy?" Nicholas' face flushed. No one knew about his father. He slapped the man hard across the face, knocking him back onto the bed.

"Shut your damn mouth! Tell me where he is or I'll see you swing for this." Hot anger flashed through him, chest heaving. The man waved a feeble hand in surrender.

"I can't tell you where he is. I don't know."

"Is he still in this prison?"

"No, he's long gone, long gone."

"How did he escape?"

"Your Da, he was real smart. I was supposed to be set loose a few months back. He let his beard grow 'til it was almost as pretty as mine. Then he gave me half his rations, starved himself to thin down like me, y'see? Even started walking and talking like me. One day, after getting some time in the yard, we just switched cells. When my time was up, it was him they let out."

"Why? What was in it for you? Are you content to be locked up here in his stead then?"

"Not likely! My name is Ezra Copeland. Now that you know you got the wrong man, you got to let me out! It's your mistake not mine."

"What did he promise you?"

"Never you mind Lawman, that's none of your business."

Nicholas' jaw worked and he gave the man a hard stare, "Josiah Cullen, goodbye and good luck." Nicholas stepped out of the cell and the guard slammed the door shut.

"What? No, now wait a minute, what are you talking about? I ain't him!" Nicholas turned to leave.

"Stop! Wait, I ain't told you everything!" He motioned Nicholas near and lowered his voice to a whisper. "He told me to tell you, don't get in his way or he'll do worse than cripple you, boy."

Nicholas gave him a cold stare before turning his back and following the guard down the hall.

* * * * *

It was late, and he was drunk. The exchange at the prison had rattled him, and he couldn't think straight. Nicholas shuffled over to the bed, toppled onto the mattress and fell into oblivion.

The next day, Nicholas ate lunch in a darkened corner of The Slaughtered Lamb. He skipped the scotch, but a pint of beer sat half-drained on the table. A dull vestige of his headache remained, but a sudden epiphany obliterated it like a bolt of lightning.

*****

"That bitch got what she deserved!" Ezra Copeland's face was red and the vein in his temple pulsed. "As soon as I got locked up, she started whoring around. Ain't no real man gonna stand for that!"

"So that was your deal, wasn't it? You would help him escape and in return, he would kill your wife."

"So you say, copper."

"He was released two days before Dora was murdered on Hawthorne Street. That's quite a coincidence, don't you think?" Ezra folded his arms and stared furiously at him.

"How long did you and your wife live on Hawthorne Street?"

"We didn't live on God-damned Hawthorne Street."

"So, where did you live?"

Ezra clamped his mouth shut before snarling, "I got nothing else to say to you."

"Shame, I thought you might be smarter than you look. Suit yourself. Take him back to his cell," he said, motioning to the guard, who led Copeland away, sputtering and cursing.

It was less than a confession, but Copeland had given him something to go on. *Where did Copeland live, and why didn't he want to tell me?*

Nicholas was still pondering when the guard returned a few minutes later, twirling his key ring.

"I need to see the warden."

* * * * *

Bourke had given orders and dozens of his gutter-urchin spies had spread out through the Lower East Side. They talked to bakers and prostitutes, factory workers and house cleaners, fishermen and petty crooks. Within the hour, the information trickled back to Bourke, and he handed Nicholas a folded note.

"That's as close as I can get you. It's a shabby place, people always coming and going, but on such short notice I can't tell you which apartment is his."

"I understand, this will do," said Nicholas.

"Now, tell me again why I shouldn't just handle this myself?" asked Bourke.

"Because this man has to face justice and you are not a police officer."

"Right. That's not even close to good enough."

"Alright then, because we made a deal. Would you go back on your word?"

"My word is as good as yours Cullen. Have it your way then. I'll take my turn when he's returned to Blackwell's."

* * * * *

McNeil Row was as blighted as any neighborhood in the Lower East Side. Bourke's note directed him to a four-story brick building with no windows on the first floor. The tenement was a beehive of activity; people flowed in and out of the entrance as thieves and pickpockets worked their way through the surrounding streets.

Nicholas loitered in the window of a dry goods store, when a man walking down the street caught his attention.

With dark hair slicked back and a trimmed beard, he stared straight ahead in a glare that caused people to move out of his way. Nicholas recognized the planes of that severe, angry face; it was Josiah Cullen, his father.

"You need any help Mister?" The storekeeper's question shocked him out of his examination. Waving away the man's question he pushed past him and walked quickly out the door.

His quarry looked neither left nor right, so it was easy to follow him into the building, taking care not to get too close. Nicholas peeked around the corner just as a door at the far end of the hallway slammed shut. *Damn! Which one was it?*

Stepping outside, he flagged down a boy of about ten with no shoes and a hard face.

"Come here, boy."

"Yes, sir?" Nicholas waved a dime in front of him.

"I need a message delivered to the Warden at Blackwell's."

* * * * *

Nicholas took up a position where he could keep the entrance under watch. Two hours passed and dusk had fallen before the boy returned.

"Your man is on his way, sir."

"Good lad. I have another job for you." Holding up another dime he said, "Find another officer and bring him to me as quick as you can." The boy snatched the coin and was off in a flash.

Within minutes, Nicholas saw the ragged figure of Ezra Copeland walking quickly through the crowd. The scrawny man shouldered his way through people, elbows pumping to either side as he rushed home.

Nicholas pulled his hat brim a little lower and walked across the street, following Copeland into the building. He slowed his pursuit enough to let Copeland get to the end of the hall, taking short, quiet steps.

Copeland tried the door, before rapping softly. "Cullen. Cullen! It's me, Ezra. Let me in." There was silence and Nicholas edged a few feet closer. He was still twenty feet away when the door cracked open and dim light spilled out. He turned away, pretending to unlock a nearby door. *Where is that officer?* Copeland hissed something inaudible before he was jerked inside the apartment, the door slamming behind him.

Taking a few deep breaths, Nicholas drew his revolver and limped over to the door. Putting his ear against it, he heard the two men arguing in angry whispers, but couldn't make out the words.

"Sir, this boy said you needed me?" The officer's voice boomed down the hallway and Nicholas cursed as the voices in the room stilled.

Retreating two steps he leaned on his cane, drew his good foot back and kicked the door as hard as he could. It burst open and he lurched into the room.

A rickety table faced the door, with a shocked Ezra Copeland to the right of it, next to a firebox with a mound of glowing coals. An oil lamp swung from a hook on the wall, and the chair at the rickety table was turned around backwards. On the left side of the table was his father.

The Butcher's hands hung at his sides. With a lowered chin, his father glared at him from under heavy brows. He looked feral, wolfish, and despite the years that had passed, Nicholas was terrified of him. His father broke the spell, turning to Copeland.

"You led him right to me, you idiot." Copeland sputtered, a dismayed look on his face that quickly turned to anger.

"Now, what's going on here?" said the officer, pushing into the room. He hadn't even drawn his revolver.

"You son-of-a-bitch!" Copeland barked at Nicholas, "I should have known you were up to something!" He snatched the poker out of the firebox and raised it.

"Don't move! I'll kill you where you stand." Nicholas was right-handed, but he couldn't hold the firearm and lean on his cane at the same time. He held the pistol in his left hand, training it on Copeland.

"Now, hold on a minute," said the officer, stepping toward Copeland. "Put that down you stupid git, before someone gets hurt." Silence held the room for a moment before Josiah spoke up.

"Look at you. Proud of yourself, eh? Preening like a rooster."

"Keep your mouth shut Cullen." Nicholas struggled to keep his composure.

"Mind your manners, boy!" Josiah seemed to swell with anger and he snarled, "Or shall I punish you again?" Nicholas flinched and swung the revolver toward the monster.

This was a mistake, I should have brought more men, he thought, but it was too late. Copeland attacked, swinging the poker and landing a savage blow across the officer's head.

He toppled like a tree, crashing into Nicholas and jarring the cane out of his grip. It clattered to the floor as he slumped back against the wall, firing a shot into Copeland's chest. Nicholas saw him fall away before a shadow flashed across his face, cracking his wrist and knocking the gun out of his hand.

He hadn't seen the hammer. His father swung the hammer at his head and Nicholas fell to the ground to avoid having his brains dashed out. Josiah pounced on top of him, but Nicholas grabbed the wrist of his hammer-hand. Josiah gripped Nicholas' throat with his free hand, an iron claw that was trying to choke him to death. The two struggled, but Josiah had gravity and ferocity on his side.

"I should have killed you long ago, you filthy little shit," he growled. Josiah leaned harder into Nicholas, putting his weight into the chokehold, causing him to gasp and wheeze. There was enormous pressure in his face and glints of light appeared at the edges of his vision. Nicholas' eyes watered and tears ran down the side of his head. His father choked him and he felt like a child again, scared and confused. The question, which had always plagued him, burst out involuntarily.

"Why…do you hate… me?" The words were choked and rasping, but the Butcher heard them.

"Why? Because your mother was a whore!" he shouted. Nicholas groped around frantically for the gun, but his hand landed on his cane instead. "Do you understand now? You're a bastard!" he roared. "You're not MY boy!" The cane was trapped beneath his bad leg, giving him the resistance he needed. Josiah slavered into Nicholas' face. "I found her though, and she died screaming!"

Something had torn inside him and Nicholas tasted blood. His eyes bulged and his face was turning purple, but he smiled a terrible smile, blood running from the corner of his mouth. *I'm NOT your boy!* He pulled the handle out, freeing the six-inch blade.

Josiah tore his wrist out of Nicholas' weakened grip and raised the hammer to strike, but the blow never fell. Nicholas had thrust the knife into his side. He ripped the blade free and thrust again. Then again, and again.

* * * * *

"Seems you forgot your cologne today," Adams whispered with a wink. It was true, Nicholas hadn't had a drink this morning. He stood next to the other detectives to receive their assignments as the Lieutenant read the cases out.

"Let's see, there was a man found in the East River, most likely a drunk. A woman was found dead when her children awoke this morning, supposedly she has taken strychnine. Lastly, two men were found dead, one knifed and one shot. Presumably an argument that got out of hand. One of our officers responded to the commotion and was killed in the melee."

Nicholas drew the drowned man, while Adams and McCarty got the other two.

Made in the USA
San Bernardino, CA
16 January 2016

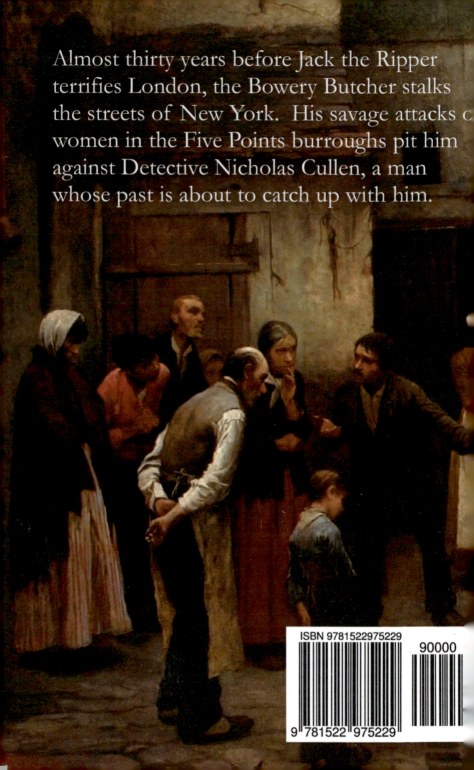

Almost thirty years before Jack the Ripper terrifies London, the Bowery Butcher stalks the streets of New York. His savage attacks on women in the Five Points burroughs pit him against Detective Nicholas Cullen, a man whose past is about to catch up with him.